MR. MAGORIUM'S WONDER EMPORIUM

Mahoney's Magic

By Mariah Balaban

SCHOLASTIC INC.

New York   Toronto   London   Auckland   Sydney
Mexico City   New Delhi   Hong Kong   Buenos Aires

walden.com/magorium and **magorium.com**

ISBN-13: 978-0-439-91248-8
ISBN-10: 0-439-91248-2

12 11 10 9 8 7 6 5 4 3 2 1   7 8 9 10/0

Book design by Rick DeMonico and Heather Barber

Printed in the U.S.A.
First printing, September 2007

Hi, my name is Eric Applebaum, and I've got a really cool story to tell. It happened at my favorite place in the world, the Wonder Emporium.

The Wonder Emporium is an amazing toy store where anything can happen and usually does. My friend Molly Mahoney is in charge now, but she wasn't always. The Wonder Emporium used to belong to Mr. Magorium.

Mr. Magorium was a toy inventor who filled the store with so much magic that the toys could play on their own. He owned the store for over a hundred years, but one day he decided that it was time for him to leave the store and the world entirely. This is the story of what happened when Mr. Magorium left, and how Mahoney took over.

It all began about a year ago. Back then, Mahoney was only the store manager. She and I were busy helping some customers when a very serious-looking man came into the store.

His name was Henry Weston, and he was an accountant. Mr. Magorium had hired him. "According to the name," Mr. Magorium said, an accountant "must be a cross between a counter and a mutant, and that may be exactly what we need!"

Henry didn't believe in magic, even when magical things happened right in front of him! Henry didn't believe in anything except his numbers. He worked all the time, and I thought that was sad.

Right after Henry showed up, I noticed things beginning to change. The store—which had once been so colorful and lively—started to turn gray. Soon after that, something even stranger happened.

The entire store went nuts! The finger paints lost all their color, the rubber balls wouldn't bounce, and a stuffed dragon breathed fire at me. The customers were freaked out, so we closed early. "The store is undergoing a little difficulty right now," I shouted. "Please leave through the front door. Calm and orderly."

After all the customers had left, Mr. Magorium called everyone together for a meeting. He told us that the store was throwing a temper tantrum. "It didn't start turning gray until Henry showed up!" I exclaimed. But Mr. Magorium said that the store was upset for a different reason.

That's when Mr. Magorium told us that he would soon be leaving forever. We were all upset, including Henry, but what Mr. Magorium said next really had us confused. He explained that he wanted Mahoney to take over the Wonder Emporium, but the store was scared that she wouldn't want it. That's why it was behaving so badly—the Wonder Emporium was sulking!

The store was right. Mahoney didn't want to be in charge. She was scared that she didn't have enough magic of her own to run it. I knew she had lots of magic in her but she needed help to find it.

In order to help her find her magic, Mr. Magorium gave Mahoney something called a Congreve Cube. It looked like a plain old block of wood, but Mr. Magorium said that it was very special. He told Mahoney, "With faith, love, this block, and a counting mutant, you may find yourself somewhere you never imagined."

Mr. Magorium and Mahoney took the day off and Henry asked if he could help out at the store. I could tell Henry was becoming more fun, because I caught him playing with the toys. That night I asked him to walk me home after work. I wanted to show him my hat collection.

When Henry saw all my hats, he was really impressed. After all, I've got almost two hundred of 'em! "Henry," I said to him, "I think we both know you wanna try a hat on." Henry picked out a jester cap, and we had a great time playing.

I was happy that Henry was my new friend, but otherwise things at the Wonder Emporium were getting worse. Mr. Magorium left for good, and Mahoney was so sad that she closed the store and put it up for sale. I visited her at her new job to try to get her to come back, but it was no use. That's when I knew it was time to take matters into my own hands.

I had to buy the Wonder Emporium. Sure, I was only nine and couldn't offer the full amount, but I had to try. I offered Henry two hundred and thirty-seven dollars, plus a check from my grandma and all of my allowances for the rest of my life. I even said I'd throw in my hat collection, but it still wasn't enough.

I begged Henry to not let Mahoney sell the store. I knew that if she sold the store she would never be able to figure out how special she is. Henry agreed that we couldn't let that happen, and he went to the Wonder Emporium to tell Mahoney she had to keep the store.

Mahoney stared at the Congreve Cube. She told Henry that the cube was supposed to help her solve a great mystery. Henry thought it was just a block of wood, but Mahoney protested. "I believe in it with all my heart," she said. Suddenly the Congreve Cube flew around the room. It really was magic, and Henry had seen it.

If the Congreve Cube needed someone to believe in its magic, then maybe that's what the Wonder Emporium needed, too! Someone to believe in it. Someone who had never believed in anything before. Someone like Henry. That's when Mahoney and I came up with our plan to save the store.

The next morning, Mahoney insisted that she hadn't seen the Congreve Cube fly, but Henry knew that he had. As he protested, the colors started coming back to the store. "It's you," Henry said to Mahoney. "You're a block of wood. You just have to believe." Suddenly Mahoney realized that just like the Congreve Cube, she could do anything as long as she believed in her magic. Then with a twinkle in her eye, Mahoney brought all the toys back to life and conducted them in a musical symphony!

And that's the story of how Mahoney discovered her magic and saved the Wonder Emporium—with a little help from me and Henry, of course. Now everything's back to normal . . . well, almost. We still miss Mr. Magorium, but Mahoney keeps the toys livelier than ever. Henry works at the store full-time, and I've even made some new friends.

Maybe when I grow up, I'll get to be in charge of the Wonder Emporium just like Mahoney. I think it will happen. After all, I've always believed in magic.